This book belongs to...

_____

Attention!
Only those who are pure of heart and love truth can travel through these pages.

Truth?

To my brother Chris, who has showed me
that there are many sides to each story.

First Greek Edition
March 2016
Translation in English
Maria Christou
Editor
Nicholas Rossis

With the kind support of
REALIZE
Via Donizetti 3, 22060 Figino Serenza (Como), Italy
Phone: +39 0315481104

Twice upon a time

Little Red Riding Hood

Author and illustrator
Marina Gioti

or Tall Tale?

A world literature classic, Little Red Riding Hood was first penned by Charles Perrault in 1697. In this original version, the story has an unhappy ending with the Big Bad Wolf eating Little Red Riding Hood—a cautionary tale of its time about the dangers of talking to strangers. The most famous version of the tale, as told by the Brothers Grimm in the 19th century, ends somewhat more happily, with the passing huntsman killing the Wolf and releasing Grandmother and Little Red Riding Hood from his stomach.

● pages: 6-19

Twice Upon a Time revisits the story of Little Red Riding Hood from a different perspective. Here, the protagonists try to look past stereotypes and newspaper headlines to discover what truly happened. What are the two sides to this story? Why does a wolf have to be bad? Why do we teach our children to stereotype from such a young age? How can we help children look beyond appearances and think critically?

● pages: 20-53

Once upon a time, there was a little girl who lived on the edge of the big woods with her mother. Everyone called her Little Red Riding Hood, because she always wore a red riding cloak; a gift from her grandmother.

One day, her mother called her and said, "Little Red Riding Hood, Granny is feeling unwell. Could you go visit and give her some cookies I've baked? But dear, please be careful. You must remember to stay away from the woods and never talk to strangers."

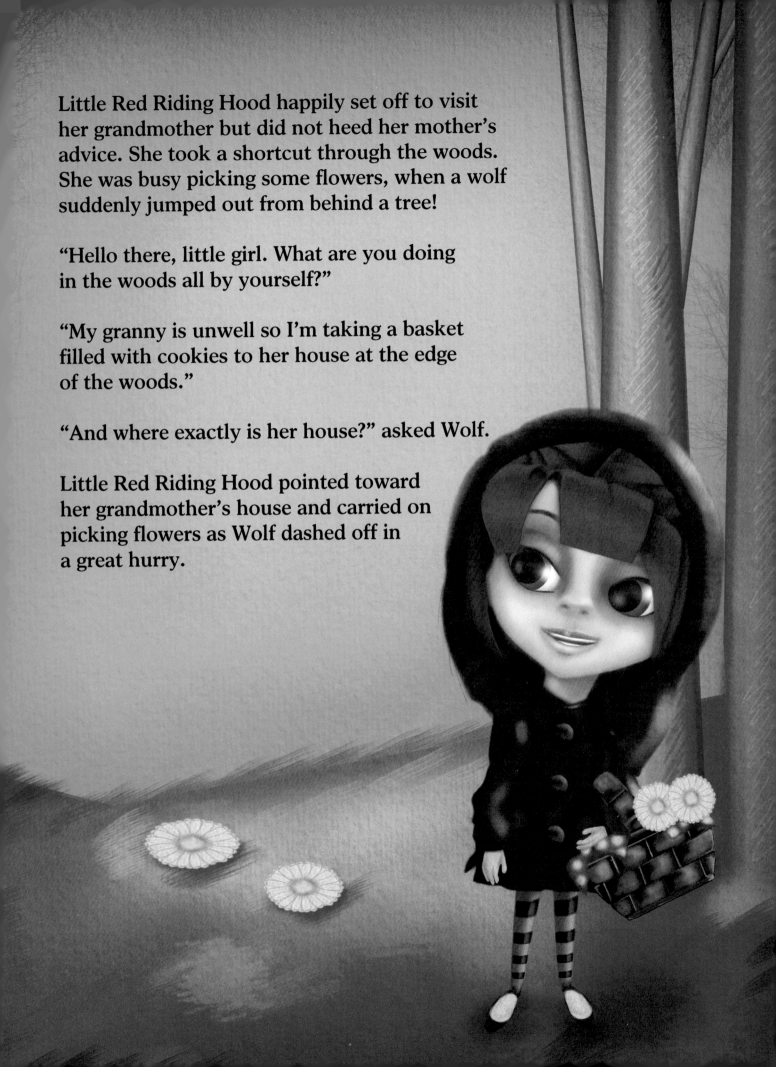

Little Red Riding Hood happily set off to visit her grandmother but did not heed her mother's advice. She took a shortcut through the woods. She was busy picking some flowers, when a wolf suddenly jumped out from behind a tree!

"Hello there, little girl. What are you doing in the woods all by yourself?"

"My granny is unwell so I'm taking a basket filled with cookies to her house at the edge of the woods."

"And where exactly is her house?" asked Wolf.

Little Red Riding Hood pointed toward her grandmother's house and carried on picking flowers as Wolf dashed off in a great hurry.

A short while later, Wolf arrived at the grandmother's
house and knocked on the front door.

"Who is it?"

the grandmother asked.

Wolf cleared his throat and spoke in
a sweet, high-pitched voice.

"It's me, Granny. I brought you a basket
of cookies Mummy baked for you."

"Little Red Riding Hood, is that you dear?
Come in, come in," said Granny.

In an instant, Wolf barged in, all ready
to gobble her up in a single bite.
Granny ran off and locked herself in the cupboard.

"That's okay, I'll eat you later," said the Wolf, dressing up in Granny's nightie.

He then burrowed under the blankets and lay in wait for Little Red Riding Hood. The little girl soon arrived. She greeted her grandmother, but something seemed not quite right.

"But Grandmother! What **big** ears you have," said Little Red Riding Hood.

"So I can hear you better, my dear," replied Wolf.

"But Grandmother! What **big** eyes you have."

"So I can see you better, my dear," replied Wolf.

"But Grandmother! What **big** teeth you have."

"So I can eat you better,"

roared Wolf and started chasing the little girl.

Little Red Riding Hood ran to the cupboard to hide and found Granny inside. They both started to run around the room, Wolf hot on their heels.

Luckily for Granny and Little Red Riding Hood, a huntsman happened to be passing through the woods at that time. He spied Wolf giving chase and rushed inside the house to stop him. The moment Wolf saw...

the huntsman's

gun

he

got such a fright that he ran

a w a y !

Little Red Riding Hood and her grandmother thanked the passing huntsman for saving their lives, and the little girl promised to never, ever again, forget her mother's words.

And they all lived

happily ever after!

Or did they?

What did really happen in the woods? Who was the mysterious huntsman and how did he happen to be at the right place at the right time? Was the Big Bad Wolf really big and really bad? What was Little Red Riding Hood doing in the woods all by herself, anyway?

Intrepid reporter Tom Flibbertigibbet was determined to read between the lines of the story.

HE FOREST NEWS

Happy ending for Little Red Riding
and her sweet grandmothe

r's advice. She took   "Who is it?" the grandmother
  She   The wolf cleared his throat
  weet, high-pitched

Exclusive News!

Ο λύκος, αφού άλλαξε τη φωνή του, είπε γλυκά: Είμαι η εγγονούλα σου και σου έφερα ένα καλάθια από τη μαμά. Αχ Κοκκινοσκουφίτσα μου, πού είσαι; Έλα μέσα, είπε η γιαγιά. Μπήκε ο λύκος, μπαίνει μέσα και με έναν πήδο... [κείμενο δυσανάγνωστο]

Η Κοκκινοσκουφίτσα άνοιξε την ντουλάπα να κρυφτεί και είδε μέσα τη γιαγιά της! Τότε άρχισαν να τρέχουν και οι δύο μέσα στο δωμάτιο, ενώ ο λύκος τις κυνηγούσε! Για κακή του τύχη όμως, εκείνη την ώρα περνούσε έξω από το σπίτι ένας κυνηγός. Είδε τον λύκο να κυνηγάει την Κοκκινοσκουφίτσα και τη γιαγιά σταμάτησε πάνω στην ώρα τον δρόμο και το δάσος τρόμαξε πολύ που το έβαλε στα πόδια.

αμέσως μετά το τρομερό συμβάν. Ο Κυνηγός δήλωσε ότι δεν υπάρχει φόβος για κανέναν, θα συνεχίσει να ψάχνει τον Λύκο και μόλις τον βρει θα φροντίσει να κανέναν ξανά. Η γιαγιά είναι εμφανώς ταλαιπωρημένη και σε κακή ψυχολογική κατάσταση και για αυτό τον λόγο δεν έχει κάνει ακόμα δηλώσεις.

Οι έρευνες συνεχίζονται χωρίς κανένα αποτέλεσμα προς το παρόν. Θα συνεχίσουμε να παρακολουθούμε το θέμα από κοντά, καθώς έχει γίνει πρώτη είδηση σε όλο το Δάσος.

The Hunter is a Hero!

Exclusive information

Στο επόμενο φύλλο της εφημερίδας μας θα ακολουθήσει ρεπορτάζ από το δάσος.

THE FOREST NEWS

Happy ending for Little Red Riding Hood and her sweet grandmother

Once upon a time there was a little girl who lived on the edge of the big woods with her mother. Everyone called her Little Red Riding Hood, because she always wore a red riding cloak, a gift from her grandmother.

One day, her mother called her and said, 'Little Red Riding Hood, Granny is feeling unwell. Cookies I baked and give her some cookies. You visit but dear, please be careful. You must remember to stay away from the woods and never talk to strangers.' Little Red Riding Hood happily set off to visit her grandmother, but did not

heed to her mother's advice. She took a shortcut through the woods! She was busy picking some flowers when a wolf suddenly jumped out from behind a tree! 'Hello there, little girl, what are you doing in the woods all by yourself?' asked the wolf. 'I'm taking a basket filled with cookies to my house,' she replied. 'Little Red Riding Hood pointed towards her house,' asked the wolf. Little Red Riding Hood pointed towards her grandmother's house and carried on picking flowers as the Wolf dashed in a great hurry to the grandmother's house and knocked on the front door.

'Who is it?' the grandmother asked. The wolf cleared his throat and spoke in a sweet, high-pitched voice. 'It's me, Granny! I brought you a basket of cookies! Mummy baked it for you,' 'Little Red Riding Hood, is that you? Granny, Come in,' said the Wolf. In an instant the Wolf lunged in, all ready to gobble her up. Granny ran off and took a hefty leap onto the cupboard. 'That's ok, I'll eat you later!' said the Wolf. He then burrowed himself in Granny's nightie and lay in wait for Little Red Riding Hood. The little girl soon arrived. She greeted her grandmother, but some

Tom carefully examined all the evidence, humming
the reporters' secret song:

Look out for the truth right now,
Find the when, who, why, and how.
Don't be fooled by the words said,
Look at the facts and think instead.
Try to keep an open mind
If you want the truth to find!

Then he set out for the woods.

Tom first tried to find the wolf's house, which proved harder than expected.

Everyone knew there was a wolf lurking around that area, but no one knew where he lived. They all called him the Big Bad Wolf and had heard many stories about him, but no one had ever really met him.

The house was at the tippy-top of the hill, right on the edge of the woods.

Tom knocked on the door…

Mrs. Wolf came to answer, her eyes all sad and gray.

"Good morning Mrs. Wolf, my name is Tom and I would like to speak to the Big Bad Wolf."

"Good morning dear," said Mrs. Wolf, somewhat suspiciously. "There is no Big Bad Wolf here. The only wolf that lived here was my son and he was good, but he left. Didn't you hear? The village people chased him away."

"Where can I find him?" Tom asked.

"I don't know. He's very shy and the village children teased him. There was this one girl, Little Red Riding Hood, who seemed nice. I could tell they wanted to be friends, but he never had the courage to talk to her. She was always with her friends and he was too shy to go up to them. He left after what happened at the grandmother's house and I haven't seen him since. If you find him, please tell him to come back; this is his home and

I love him very much!"

Tom pensively bade Mrs. Wolf farewell and headed off toward Little Red Riding Hood's house. It looked like things were not as they seemed.

He had to speak with her as soon as possible.

He found Little Red Riding Hood on her swing in the garden, her grandmother baking in the kitchen.

"Hello, Little Red Riding Hood," Tom said.
"Can I ask you a few questions?"

"Mummy told me not to talk to strangers. I didn't listen to her last time and I don't want to make that mistake again," she answered abruptly.

"My name is Tom. I'm a reporter, I write for The Forest News."

"I know you," exclaimed the little girl.
"My dad reads your newspaper and sometimes grumbles about what you write."

"I would like to learn more about the Big Bad Wolf," said Tom.

"Why would you?"

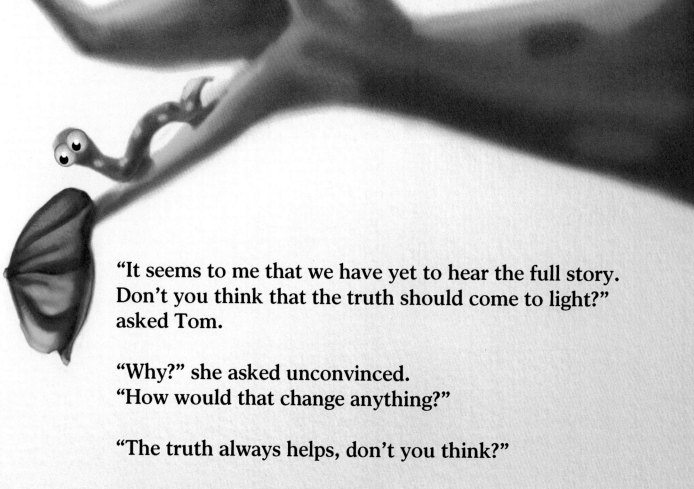

"It seems to me that we have yet to hear the full story. Don't you think that the truth should come to light?" asked Tom.

"Why?" she asked unconvinced.
"How would that change anything?"

"The truth always helps, don't you think?"

"Helps who? Helps you and your newspaper, because it gives you something to write about."

"The truth is good for everyone, Little Red Riding Hood; the truth helps what's right and fights what's wrong."

"Okay, what if I told you that the Big Bad Wolf isn't actually bad; would you believe me? Or would you say that I'm too young to understand?"

"Of course I would believe you. That's why I'm here, to actually listen to what you have to say."

Little Red Riding Hood looked at him for a minute undecided. Finally she cried out,

"Alright then, I'll tell you!"

"I'm the one who asked him to run ahead to Granny's house and tell her I would be late. I know Wolf from school. I'd see him sit at his desk alone all day long and no one ever spoke to him.

When I saw him walking through the forest, I worked up the courage to speak with him. He was nice and very sweet and we got carried away talking about so many interesting things that I lost track of time."

"What happened next?" Tom asked, jotting everything down in his notebook.

"I was already late and he is the faster runner, so I begged him to run over to Granny's to let her know.

He was so happy to help me."

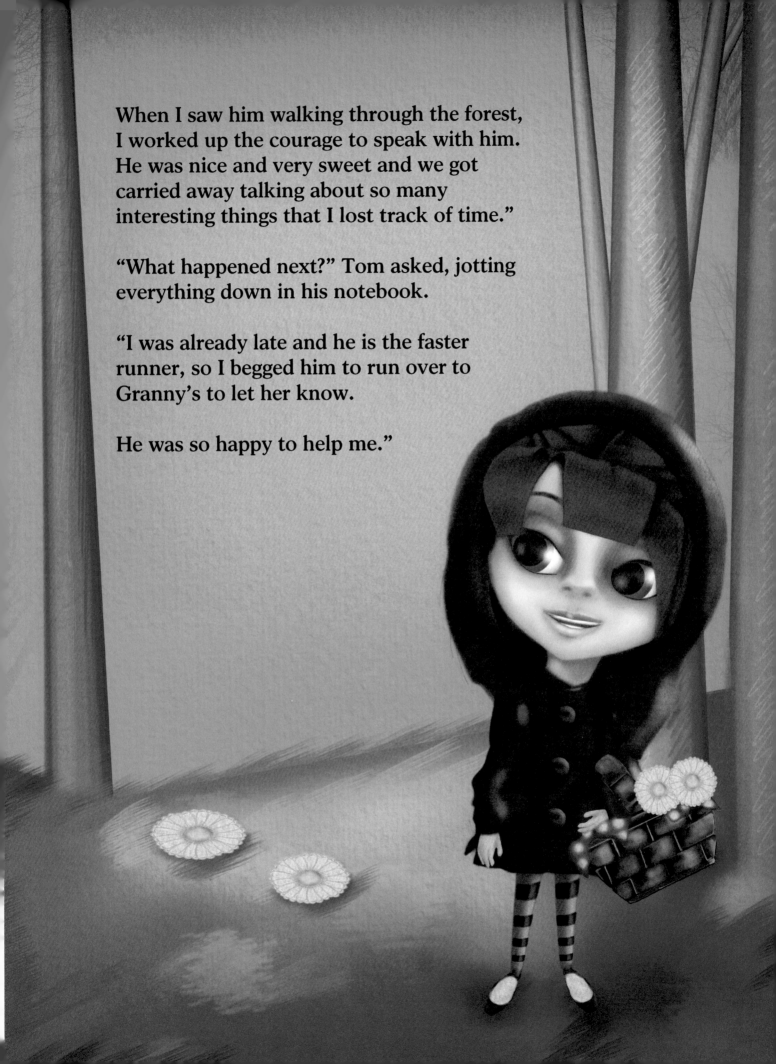

"When I got to the house, I found Granny in the cupboard and Wolf sitting on the bed, looking really sad. I asked him what had happened and he told me that when Granny saw him she got scared, locked herself in the cupboard and refused to come out.

We tried to reason with her. We told her a wolf's just like a puppy and that there was no reason for her to be afraid. To show Granny just how sweet Wolf could be, he put on her nightie, but that didn't really make any difference."

"But if you are like a puppy, why do you have such

big ears?" she asked.
"So I can hear you better."
"And why do you have such

big eyes?"
"So I can see you better."
"And why do you have such

big teeth?"

This bothered him a little, because he's a bit sensitive about the size of his teeth.

"So I can eat you better!"

he said, trying to tease her.

Now that I think about it, that wasn't very smart of him, because Granny jumped right out of the cupboard and started screaming. She ran frantically around the room and we went after her to calm her down. That's when Mr. Huntsman showed up…"

39

Grandmother came out of the kitchen. She had overheard everything Little Red Riding Hood and Tom had discussed.

"I had heard so many awful things about the Big Bad Wolf that I started running without really thinking about it. Rumors and half-truths, I imagine, from people who have never even met him."

"It often happens," Tom said,

"to fear  what we do not know."

Little Red Riding Hood continued,
"Before I knew it, that Huntsman was shouting,

"The Big Bad Wolf
wants to gobble up
Little Red Riding Hood.

RUN!"

And he took out his gun. A crowd had gathered and everyone was shouting. Then my friend, Wolf, realized that he was in a whole lot of trouble and ran away. Mr. Huntsman went after him, loading his shotgun.

I tried to stop them, but no one could hear me over all the noise and shouting.

Luckily, Wolf managed to run away and hide in the woods. Eventually, we managed to calm down Granny and the whole village congratulated Mr. Huntsman. No one would listen to me because they all thought I was in shock!"

"Still hiding somewhere in the woods," Little Red Riding Hood replied. "Only Granny knows where he is. At night, she brings him food and water. He has no idea how to survive in the woods on his own. Imagine, that's how savage he is."

Tom nonetheless had a hunch he still hadn't learned the whole truth. Something was missing.

How did Mr. Huntsman happen to arrive at the grandmother's house at that very moment? The window did not overlook the road, so how did he see Wolf? And why did he have his gun with him, if he wasn't going hunting?

"How strange!"

he mumbled, his mind already racing.

He thanked Little Red Riding Hood and her grandmother and walked back to the village.

Tom went to the library at the other end of the village, and once inside headed straight to the archive of old newspaper clippings. He searched and searched and sometime later found what he was looking for.

It looked like Mr. Huntsman had been busy in other villages as well, always looking for a wolf with a beautiful coat of fur.

He would **scare** the villagers with stories about how big and bad the wolf was, then hunt him down for his fur.

The trick always worked because, even though wolf hunting was banned, no one ever spoke up. Instead, people called him a hero and thanked him for saving them!

Tom decided to reveal the hunter's plot and started writing down the whole truth in a tell-all article. He had almost finished when there was a knock at the door.

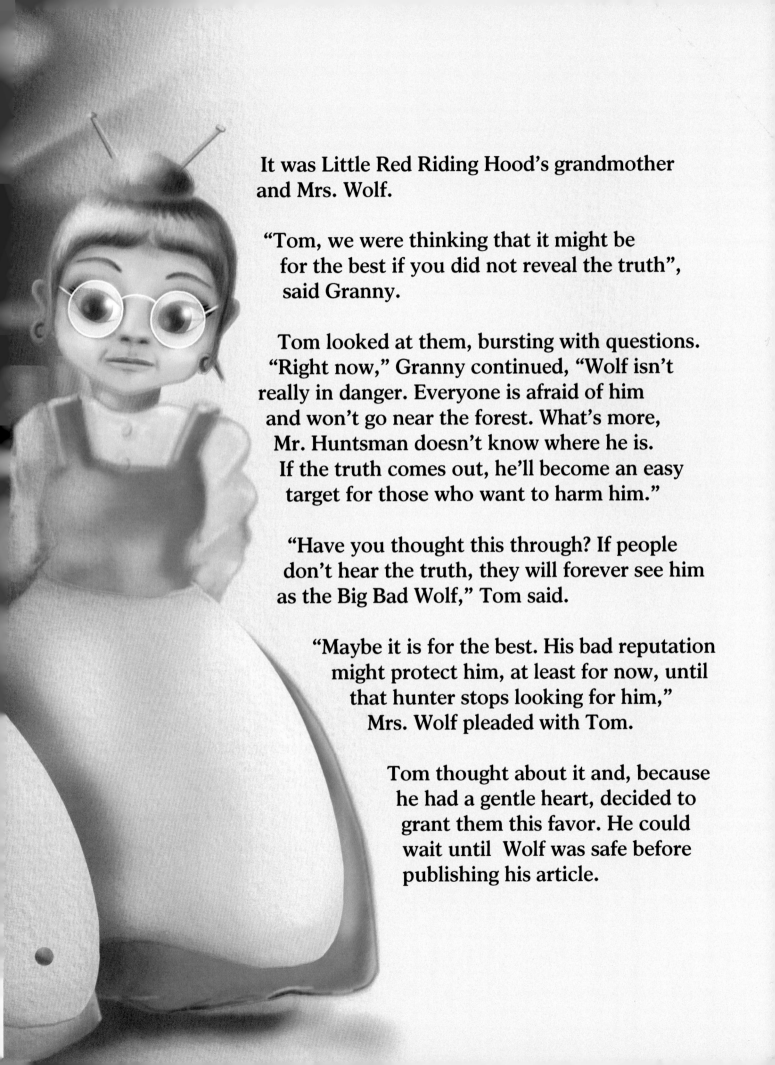

It was Little Red Riding Hood's grandmother and Mrs. Wolf.

"Tom, we were thinking that it might be for the best if you did not reveal the truth", said Granny.

Tom looked at them, bursting with questions. "Right now," Granny continued, "Wolf isn't really in danger. Everyone is afraid of him and won't go near the forest. What's more, Mr. Huntsman doesn't know where he is. If the truth comes out, he'll become an easy target for those who want to harm him."

"Have you thought this through? If people don't hear the truth, they will forever see him as the Big Bad Wolf," Tom said.

"Maybe it is for the best. His bad reputation might protect him, at least for now, until that hunter stops looking for him," Mrs. Wolf pleaded with Tom.

Tom thought about it and, because he had a gentle heart, decided to grant them this favor. He could wait until Wolf was safe before publishing his article.

Time passed and Wolf lived safe and happy in the forest. Everyone feared him and did not come near.

Little Red Riding Hood would visit Wolf every day and read and play with him. They even told a few trusted friends and let them come along. As time went by, the children no longer cared what people said.

They knew who they were, and whether people thought they were good or bad, tall or short, smart or silly, pretty or ugly mattered not one bit!

The real story of Wolf is kept in the book Tom wrote, Twice upon a Time was Little Red Riding Hood. It is a magical book that can only be read by those who are pure of heart, so as to protect Wolf from the world's unkindness. That is how this book has now found its way to you.

Twice upon a time

Little Red Riding Hood
The true story

Tom Flibbertigibbet

Is he wearing a hat or glesses

Initial Drawing

Ink and color

Final sketch

Other views

Μαρίνα Τσώτη

Marina Gioti Bio

Children's books and art are Marina Gioti's twin passions; passions that have found their perfect expression in her best-selling children's books. Born in Athens, Greece, Marina studied Marketing and Fine Arts at Georgetown University in Washington, D.C. followed by Communication Design at Pratt Institute in N.Y.

She is the 1999 recipient of the John Peter's Publication Award and Scholarship from the N.Y. Art Directors Club and has won a Bronze Pentaward for her work in design. Her book, "Twice upon a time - Little Red Riding Hood," was voted as one of the 10 best picture books in her native Greece (2016).

Marina spends her time between Greece and the UK, writing, illustrating and giving book presentations to children and parents. She is a regular contributor to popular magazines and websites.

You can contact Marina:

🖱 marina@marinagioti.gr
f Marina Gioti
🐦 Marina Gioti
📷 marina_gioti
in Marina Gioti
www.marinagioti.gr

Thank you for taking the time to read Twice Upon a Time: Little Red Riding Hood.
If you enjoyed it, please tell your friends or post a short review on Amazon or Goodreads.
Word of mouth is an author's best friend and much appreciated!

Find out more about marina and her books at

www.marinagioti.gr

Made in the USA
Middletown, DE
15 January 2018